BRINDLE BOOKS

http://www.brindlebooks.co.uk

Unseen Follower

By

Sophia Moseley

Brindle Books Ltd 2023

Brindle Books Ltd

Copyright © 2023 by Sophia Moseley

This edition published by
Brindle Books Ltd
Unit 3, Grange House
Grange Street
Wakefield
United Kingdom
WF2 8TF
Copyright © Brindle Books Ltd 2023

The right of Sophia Moseley to be identified as author of this work has been asserted by her in accordance with the Copyright, Designs and Patents Act 1988.
ISBN 978-1-915631-14-5

All rights reserved. No part of this publication may be reproduced, stored in a retrieval system or transmitted, in any form or by any means, electronic, mechanical, photocopying, recording or otherwise without the prior permission of the Copyright holder

CONTENTS

Unseen Follower

Case Study

"To flatter and follow others, without being flattered and followed in turn, is but a state of half enjoyment."

Jane Austen

Unseen Follower

'Last year, 63.1 percent of divorces were instigated by women and 36.9 by men. What does that tell you?'

Caroline pushed her sunglasses to the top of her head, pinning her long dark hair away from her face, turned to look at Sam, her oldest and closest friend, and said, 'That the male population really are incapable of seeing what's staring them in the face?'

'No, Caroline,' said Sam. 'What that tells you is there are a lot of single women out there, all after the same blokes – and whilst men seem to be okay staying in a rubbish marriage, women are most definitely not. But that means there aren't going to be many men left out there for the likes of you.'

'Maybe it's an omen,' Caroline said.

'*What?*'

'All those numbers, lots of sixes. It was six years with Neil, the last six months of which were hell, then six weeks with Karl. Six, six, six … maybe someone's trying to tell me something.'

'Or it could be a case of third time lucky, so the next one'll be the *one*,' replied Sam.

'That too. But either way, right now I don't want to think about men or dating.'

'You say that now,' said Sam, 'but I know what you're like, and as much as you believe in fate and keep thinking you're literally going to bump into Mr Right one day, if you joined one of the dating sites you could take control of your destiny and find the perfect match.'

Caroline sighed. 'Maybe, but I don't want to think about it right now. I'm so glad we did this. I've enjoyed not having to think about anything or anyone for a few days.' She slipped her sunglasses back down onto the bridge of her nose and sat up, crossing her legs in front of her. She looked out across the huge expanse of Mediterranean Sea that stretched to the horizon. The sea was so calm and flat, it looked like someone had drawn a perfect straight line between the cobalt blue of the sky and the deep blue of the sea. The air still felt fresh – it was late spring – but in just over a month not only would the weather have changed to the more familiar intense heat, but the deserted stretch of golden sand they had to themselves would be colonised by crowds of holidaymakers, each of them commandeering their strip of beach, eyeing up the pale newcomers with that tanned and pitying derision of the week-long seasoned residents they had become.

'I wish we could stay here for ever, freeze this moment in time, never get older, never tire of this idyllic location, just keep enjoying each minute of sun-kissed bliss,' Caroline said.

Sam put her magazine down. 'It *is* nice, isn't it? But real life awaits, there's no escaping it, and until you write your bestseller or finally find a way to make it pay to be a freelance journo – or my practice gets taken over by a multinational for a huge amount of money – we both need to get back to work. Come on, let's go for a last swim.'

She stood up and stretched, luxuriating in the joy of the deserted beach, and not having to worry about anyone looking at her and thinking she'd had a few too many second helpings. Having vowed some years earlier that she'd never be seen dead in a swimsuit, now, with just the two of them there, it was liberating for her to wear so little and not care, and whilst Caroline could still fit into the same size jeans she had when she was sixteen, Sam's size didn't matter to her, because the two of them had always valued their friendship above all else.

Caroline looked up at Sam and grinned. 'Race you,' she said, as she pushed herself up off the lounger, and they both ran the short distance between the shade of the trees and the crystal-clear water. The smooth surface of the sea erupted into a fountain of salty splashes as their legs broke into the water until they were knee deep and had to slow down. They skidded their hands over the surface, showering each other, until they were waist deep, then threw themselves into the glittering sea. Caroline sculled lazily on her back, lying flat so her hair floated around her like a bed of rich dark kelp.

It was only when their holiday rep appeared on the shore and pointed at her watch that they reluctantly made their way back onto the beach and walked back to the loungers, the sand sticking to their feet.

They'd had to check out of their rooms at ten that morning, but as the flight was not until three o'clock in the afternoon, they had decided to make the most of every minute and had taken their bags down to the beach. They wouldn't be able to shower before they headed to the plane, but they didn't care, even if it meant they would be flying back with the tingle of seawater on their skin and sand still between their flip-flopped toes.

The rep stood close by and impatiently reminded them there was just the one flight back, and if they missed it there was nothing for three days. She also suggested they might want to find something a bit warmer to wear as the temperature in London was around seven degrees, and their sun dresses might not be the best choice. Caroline looked at Sam and rolled her eyes. The rep was quite a bit older than them and had a bit of a matronly way about her.

'We're all right, don't worry,' Caroline said, as they took one last look at the sea, then picked up their cases to follow the rep to the waiting taxi.

As they boarded the plane an hour later and found their seats, Caroline turned to Sam and said, 'Okay, I'll give the dating idea a go. Maybe I could write up about my experiences, sell it to one of the trashy magazines you read: '*The diary of an online dater.*'

'Great idea!' said Sam, laughing. 'It might be interesting, and fun – and you never know, you could meet the man of your dreams. But you have to be honest about yourself, and about the kind of person you want to meet. Do you remember those lists we used to write at school, of what we did and didn't want in a boyfriend?'

'I'd forgotten all about those!' Caroline said, 'I think I still have mine somewhere. That would be a great start to the article – *the pre-social media teenage dream in an online adult world.*'

As the Boeing 737 taxied down the runway, the two of them laughed at their memories of teenage prerequisites when it came to boyfriends, and how things had turned out for them both – and whilst Sam, at nearly thirty-one, was happy to stay single, Caroline was not. What Sam had said was undoubtedly true; as each year passed, she knew the odds diminished of finding someone to share her life with. But was that what she really wanted? Maybe she should try being happy on her own. It was certainly less hassle. At least it meant her bathroom was never cluttered with cans of shaving foam and spent razors left on the side, or a ring of stubble residue in the basin or nail clippings and dirty footprints in the bath. There was definitely a lot to be said about living on your own, but on the other hand the quiet and solitude did sometimes get a bit depressing. After all, having someone to bounce ideas off, or to moan to about her day at work, or sitting in the back row of the cinema with and not worrying about missing most of the film, was more fun than giving herself a pep-talk in the bathroom mirror, which she had found herself doing more often of late.

But after six years with Neil, the last six months filled with disagreements and each blaming the other for the smallest of incidents, and then the six weeks with Karl, she wasn't sure if another person in her life was what she wanted right now.

As the plane levelled out and the seatbelt sign went off, they started to write out a new list of must-have and must-not-haves. By the time they landed at Gatwick Airport two hours later they had four pages of notes.

∞∞

Sam and Caroline had known each other since primary school. Their mums had joked they were so well tuned into each other's way of thinking, they must be psychic twins. So, when Caroline had phoned Sam that Sunday afternoon to ask if she'd go with her asap to an island a long way from anyone and everything, Sam knew things must be bad, because Caroline never did anything on the spur of the moment.

'By the sound of things,' said Sam, 'we need to talk, especially if what's happened is what I thought would happen. Come round to mine at six. I'll get the pizza and wine.'

Caroline arrived at Sam's front door that evening. The warm glow of love that had radiated from Caroline's face since she had met Karl six weeks earlier had now turned into the red of rage.

Sam put her arm round her shoulders as she pushed the door shut behind her. 'Tell me what happened, then I'll send the boys round to sort him out.' Right on cue, two excitable miniature terriers came hurtling out of the lounge to see what all the fuss was about. 'There, you see, they're ready to do what's needed – though I'm not sure their definition of a good licking is quite the same as mine.'

Caroline snuffled a feeble laugh as she bent down to stroke their heads, satisfying their demand for attention, and they trotted behind the two women back into the lounge, their claws tip-tapping on the wooden floor.

The lounge was warm and welcoming. One wall was lined with bookshelves that heaved under the weight of every book Sam had been given since she was in kindergarten, including several first editions. A small dining table sat neatly in the arc of the bay window at one end, and opposite it, French doors looked out onto a small, picturesque garden just starting to show signs of life after the winter. On the mantelpiece were several awards for her achievements as a clinical animal behaviourist; her ability to discover what caused certain traits in animals was something she often applied to humans, and she rarely got it wrong. Her compassion and understanding were the signature of her success – even her lounge seemed to open its arms to Caroline as she walked in and put her bag on the floor next to the well-loved shabby sofa that cocooned her with squishy cushions and a warm soft throw draped over the back. A small coffee table sat neatly between the sofa and an equally well-worn armchair opposite, the mismatched style and colour adding to the general warmth and ambience of the room.

Sam put two filled wine glasses on the table, then said, 'Come on, then, tell me what happened.'

Caroline lifted her glass and took several sips as she tried to work out what to say first. 'You were right – well almost, not entirely, but pretty much.'

Sam waited patiently as Caroline took gulps rather than sips until her glass was virtually empty.

'I wish I could be like you,' said Caroline, 'and see through all the crap, and stop missing the obvious.'

Sam was used to Caroline's cryptic opening sentences, and the way she would circumnavigate her way round a topic before getting to the point. It never ceased to amaze her that Caroline managed to get any of her editing work completed within deadlines.

'There are always good bits and bad bits,' Sam replied as she refilled Caroline's glass. 'No matter what or who it is. The problem is when you have someone who's a serial liar, and I'm afraid that's what he is.'

Caroline took another gulp, then rummaged around in her bag. 'I switched it off in case he tried to call or message me,' she said as she pressed the button on the side of her iPhone.

'I can't believe that old thing still works after you dropped it in the bath. I thought you were going to get a new one,' Sam said as she settled back into the armchair, pulling her legs up to one side and resting her elbow on the arm.

'It seemed to be all right after I dried it out, though the battery doesn't last as long as it did, and the cracked screen is a pain. Anyway, here it is – listen.' Caroline read the message she had screenshotted: *Looking forward to seeing you tonight, sorry I can't be with you this afternoon, I couldn't get out of the appointment I told you about, but we can make it extra special tonight, celebrate our six-month anniversary xx*

'But it's not *me* he's seeing tonight – it was me who was his '*afternoon appointment*'! It was sheer chance I saw it the moment he'd sent it, and when I read it and realised what was going on, I took the screenshot, so he couldn't deny it. He deleted the message within minutes, but he'll know I've read it, the tick would've turned blue.'

Caroline passed her phone to Sam so she could see it for herself, as if seeing it was greater proof than just hearing it.

∞∞

Sam had seen this coming for several days and had tried to warn Caroline about the likelihood that Karl was still seeing his old girlfriend. He had a reputation in Aylsham, the small Norfolk market town where they lived, and having met him at one of the pub quiz nights she fully understood how Caroline had been captivated by his wit and charm, and by his lopsided grin that he had perfected and swore blind was due to being kicked in the face during a school rugby match – which also explained, he said, why he had one blue and one hazel eye. He was handsome in an unconventional way, and saying how his being 'damaged goods' affected his self-esteem made him all the more desirable. Which was why there was never a shortage of women who intended to usurp his existing girlfriend in the hope they would be the one.

After finishing her relationship with Neil, Caroline had been left so emotionally exhausted that she wasn't looking for love, and whilst she'd seen Karl around and knew about him, she hadn't paid him any attention – in fact she'd completely blanked him a couple of times. And it was that that had made her attractive to him. Especially as his current girlfriend was going on a long-haul trip, and he was looking for someone to fill the gap.

So, when he saw Caroline on her own in the launderette one afternoon, he put on his best little-boy-lost appearance as he walked through the door and told her he had been sent by his gran to collect her laundry because it was too far for her to walk.

In that moment, it was like she was seeing him for the first time. She recognised him as she'd seen him around town, but as he pushed open the heavy door and looked straight into her eyes she was mesmerised.

Within minutes of him asking her to help him locate a missing pile of his granny's flannelette nighties, all she could see were his pleading eyes. Her desire seemed to override her sense of reason, and she became coquettish in their game of find-the-missing-granny-garments. It didn't occur to her that each machine was empty other than the one she was using, and she surprised herself at how long it took her to decide an empty washing machine was indeed empty, as she crouched down and peered inside the huge empty drum, rising slowly each time to within inches of his face. By the time they reached the sixth and final machine, Caroline would have been happy to wash his entire wardrobe by hand had he asked.

Having lost all sense of reason that afternoon and agreed to go out with him for a meal that evening, she broke her cardinal rule for first dates; before the end of even the first course they were paying the bill and couldn't get back to her place quickly enough.

Later that night, she sent a WhatsApp to Sam: *I'm with an #Adonis*

Caroline longed to fall asleep in his arms to the sound of their gentle slow breathing as their bodies slipped into grateful sleep, the warmth of their skin fusing them together, their synchronised desire and passion satiated, leaving them utterly content to just lie together.

As she lay her head on his smooth hairless chest, listening to his heartbeat slowly return to normal, her left hand resting on his sixpack of a stomach, Karl twisted a coil of her long hair around his fingers, his other hand resting on her thigh. 'You have beautiful hair, it's so soft, and smells nice. Bit like you, you're soft and smell nice.'

Caroline lifted her head and kissed him. 'Thank you. You're not. That is, not soft, I mean, but you smell nice.'

He laughed and rolled her over on her back, then propped himself up on his elbow so he could look into her eyes. 'I like you, Caroline, I like you a lot, and I'd like to see you again, soon. Can I?'

'I like you too, Karl, very much – and yes, I'd like that. Though you don't have to go now, you can stay the night if you want.' She hoped she didn't sound too desperate, but as he threw back the duvet, she knew it wasn't going to happen.

'Would love to, but I have to go to work – I'm on the nightshift this week. I'll text you later if that's okay,' Karl said as he pulled on his jeans, 'and let's keep this between us, I mean you and me. I don't like people knowing my business, and you know what it's like in this town for gossip.'

Caroline watched him as he pulled the skin-tight T-shirt over his head, and whilst she was fascinated by his faultless torso it suddenly occurred to her that she knew absolutely nothing about him, not even where he worked. She had indeed managed to break every rule in her book of first dates in one fell swoop.

He put one knee on the bed and bent down to kiss her goodbye, and whispered, 'Soft and sweet,' in her ear.

After he had gone, Caroline lay staring up at her bedroom ceiling, going over everything in the last few hours, trying to work out how it had happened. And whilst he'd said he wanted to keep it secret, Caroline *had* to talk to someone, so she rang Sam, and the conversation was just as she expected: was she mad? didn't she know he had a reputation? had she forgotten their conversation about taking a dating break after Neil? and what was she doing, anyhow, breaking the cardinal rule that they'd both agreed – no sex on a first date?

'I know, I know,' she pleaded, 'but he's everything Neil wasn't, and I know it won't last, and I know all the other stuff. I'm just having a bit of fun.'

'Just be careful,' Sam said. 'There are more broken hearts in his wake than fish in the sea.'

'I know. I'm under no illusion,' Caroline said, perhaps trying to persuade herself more than anything.

Over the next few days, Karl messaged Caroline often and saw her when he could. By week three she was beginning to think maybe he was the one, and that she must mean something to him, or why would he say the things he did? And on the odd occasion he had to change arrangements at the last minute, she would tell herself she had nothing to worry about. That was until six weeks after their first meeting in the launderette, when her phone pinged with *that* WhatsApp from him – and when she read it, despite having told Sam she was under no illusions, her heart sank. Which was why she'd taken a screenshot of the message.

Sam was careful not to say, 'I told you so', because she could see how upset Caroline was. What she said instead was, 'If he shows up at the next quiz night, I'll make sure I accidentally on purpose spill my pint all over him.' The doorbell rang and a courier delivered two huge pizza boxes. By the end of the evening and another bottle of wine, Caroline was almost back to her old self, and they'd booked the trip to the Greek island.

∞∞

'Here you are; this one's perfect,' Sam said as she passed her phone to Caroline, who looked at the profile picture and read the description. It was fortnight since their week in the Med, though it seemed like a lifetime away, and the golden glow of their suntan had virtually faded to nothing. They were sitting in Caroline's kitchen with a plate of Danish pastries and a pot of coffee.

'I don't know, Sam, I'm having second thoughts. I mean it's just not *me*, is it, online dating? It's just so, I don't know ... desperate. I feel like a prize heifer being inspected before someone decides I'm worth it.'

'It's not at all like that – well, okay, maybe a little – but it's just a bit of fun, and Tony's given a tick of approval to your request to chat.'

Caroline frowned, 'What request? I haven't made a request.'

'No – but I did, on your behalf. I signed up for you this morning, and you've already had thirty-five visits to your profile – and this one ticks every box. You've told him you'd like to chat. You can thank me later.'

Sam swung the laptop round so Caroline could see Tony's full profile. He certainly looked interesting and ticked a lot of the boxes on her wish-list. He was an artist currently working on a project near where he lived in Manchester. 'All right,' Caroline said, 'just to humour you, I'll call him.'

A couple of days later, Caroline was relaying to Sam the conversation she'd had with Tony. He had been in a Waterstones bookshop café taking a break from his research when she had phoned. He told her he was enjoying a Cadbury's Fruit & Nut bar whilst drinking a large coffee, and that he was a bit of a chocoholic.

She said he'd gone on to explain why he was in the bookshop; he was looking for some specific books. Sam was beginning to think he sounded the perfect match for her friend. Then Caroline said that he'd added that the titles of the books weren't important – it was the size and colour that were essential – and he needed roughly two hundred and fifty of them.

'A little unusual,' Sam remarked, 'but maybe he has a walk-in library at home he needs to fill.'

'I haven't finished. It gets better,' Caroline said. 'He told me that once he's found enough books, he's going to create something like an upside-down pyramid, with some book spines facing out so the titles show, and some on their side, others laid flat, some open, some shut. It'll be a gigantic interlocking literary sculpture. But it isn't going to be in an art gallery, or part of some exciting contemporary exhibition – it's going to be built in a hangar on a disused airstrip, the location being of equal importance.' She paused for dramatic effect, as she described the huge mountain of books, each chosen to ensure they fitted into the top-heavy shape. Sam waited, intrigued to know what his plan was. 'And then,' Caroline continued, 'after he's sure each book is in just the right place, that the shading's exactly right, the shape's just as he wants – then he'll set the whole thing on fire.'

Sam nearly spat out her coffee.

'But it doesn't end there,' said Caroline. 'It gets better.'

Sam put her cup down, not wanting to make a mess. 'Go on, don't tell me – the fire brigade will arrive and ruin the whole thing.'

'Who knows? I kind of glazed over at that point. But then he asked about my writing, so I told him a few things I'd done, which is when he told me about *his* latest story. The bits I remember included him running naked through a field of ripe corn – him, and the woman he was with, having rampant sex then making corn angels. By this time, all I could think about was how painful it must be to get a branch of corn stuck somewhere, and to be honest, I'm not sure if it was a story he was telling me about, or some weird fantasy of his.'

Tears of laughter rolled down Sam's cheeks. 'Well, don't be put off – that was just the first one. There must be *some* who are normal. You just need to find them.'

Caroline filled her mug again and took another pastry. 'I think I'll put the whole idea on the backburner for the time being – and anyway, I've been given a new commission, an article on local hero Joseph Thomas Clover. A pioneer in anaesthesia, and he's been dead for over a hundred and thirty years. That's much less dangerous than a pyromaniac with a penchant for chocolate and corn dollies!'

∞∞

Caroline's new commission meant she had no time to think about men or relationships, and whilst she hadn't deleted the online dating account, she ignored the friend requests and messages. Which is why, when a Facebook friend request pinged onto her screen, whilst she vaguely recognised the sender, she couldn't recall where from, so she deleted the request. Having written articles about women being stalked and trolled, she wasn't going to let someone do the same to her.

A few days later as she was coming out of the library with a toppling pile of reference books, she bumped into someone heading into the building. As they collided, one of her books slipped and fell to the floor.

'Here, let me help.' His voice was as rich and dark as molasses.

'Oh, thank you. Sorry, I wasn't watching where I was going, I hope I didn't walk into you,' Caroline said, as he picked the book up and put it back on the pile she was carrying.

'Have you got far to go? That's a lot of books to carry,' he said, smiling at her.

'That's all right, I don't have far to walk. My car's just over there.' Caroline smiled back, feeling she recognised him from somewhere. 'Don't I know you?'

'Not exactly. I follow you on Facebook – I'm Chris – and you've probably seen me around. I've had quite a few jobs since my redundancy, keeping the wolf from the door and all that.'

Then she remembered the friend request, and suddenly felt guilty. 'Oh yes, I'm sorry, I remember now – I don't follow you back, do I?'

'That's okay, I don't expect you to. Anyway, let me help, it's no bother. Here, I'll take those top few books, then you can at least get your car keys out.'

Caroline unlocked the boot and wedged her books in amongst boxes of more books and magazines.

'You have a lot of reading to do,' he said as Caroline took the remaining books from him.

'You could say that, it's kind of what I do. Anyway, thanks for helping.'

'No problem, see you around.' He adjusted the strap of his rucksack and slipped his phone back into his jeans pocket, smiled, headed back over the road to the library and disappeared. Caroline watched as the doors slowly slid shut behind him. *And they say chivalry's dead,* she thought to herself. She was just about to close the boot of her car when she noticed her phone on top of the books he'd carried for her. *That's odd,* she thought, *I don't remember putting it there.* She slipped it back into the front pocket of her bag.

For the rest of the day and late into the evening, she pored over the library books, making copious notes. Research was one of the aspects of Caroline's job she loved, and she would leave no stone unturned to make sure she had every possible bit of information, and as this article was for a nationally recognised journal, she had to make 100 per cent sure it was accurate. By the time she'd finished it was nearly midnight, so she drained her wine glass and went to bed.

Before she fell asleep, she went through her deleted friend requests, to find the one Chris had sent, but the phone wouldn't renew the option to accept it, so she clicked on his profile and sent a friend request to him. Within minutes he'd confirmed it. *That's a bit keen,* she thought, noticing the little green dot next to his profile picture. It unnerved her slightly – she felt like she'd been caught out, because it meant he was online at the same time as her. She switched her phone off then plugged it into the charger.

When she woke the next morning and reached out for her phone as usual, she was surprised to find it wasn't where she expected. Instead of lying face down next to her bed, where she thought she'd left it, it was on the floor, facing up and switched on. She thought it a bit odd, but realised she couldn't have switched it off properly, and then must have knocked it onto the floor in the night.

She got up and made herself a coffee, grabbed the Sunday papers from the doormat, and went back to bed planning to read them – but then, instead, clicked on the Facebook icon on her phone. *Where's the harm?* she thought to herself as she scrolled through his Facebook feed. *If people don't want their details looked at or their posts read, then they shouldn't put them up.*

But after scrolling through his posts, Caroline couldn't decide whether or not she was disappointed at how dull they were: a few pictures of a football game, some sporting memes, and a couple of links to political news. She clicked on the profiles of a few of the people who had commented on or liked his posts, but most of them didn't have public pages, so all she could see were a few profile picture updates. There were a couple of check-ins he had added, including one of her favourite restaurants; and a wine-tasting evening she'd been interested in was listed under his Events.

His profile status said he was single, but not whether that was due to divorce, being widowed or anything else. So, not exactly a man of complete mystery, but not much to go on, either.

Her phone pinged, telling her someone had messaged her, and she tapped on the icon, expecting it to be Sam or her mum reminding her about where she was meant to be going that day – but when she opened it, she was so surprised she said 'Oh!' out loud.

∞∞

Morning. I hope you slept well and are enjoying a relaxing morning. It's going to be a beautiful sunny day. I hope you will manage a few minutes away from your research to enjoy it. Have a nice day.

There was nothing she could do about it. Chris'd know straight away she'd read it – but more to the point, he'd know she was online. It hadn't occurred to her that he'd message her. She tapped the home button to take her to the main screen. She might have read his message straight away, but she wasn't going to respond to it as quickly. So she put her phone down and opened Facebook on her laptop.

When she had bought the laptop, she had asked her IT genius brother to set it up so she could browse anonymously, which made everything much easier. So now she scrolled through Chris's posts again, this time confident he wouldn't know she was online. She tapped on the images of a couple of his friends – again there was nothing remarkable. Comments about football, cricket, films, and beer, so all pretty blokeish. She carried on scrolling through until she realised she'd been searching his timeline for nearly half an hour. She thought about the last article she had written for a student magazine, called *The Infinite Scroll*, which explained how people got hooked on social media, and she was about to tap on the home icon when she saw an image of him with a very attractive younger woman, and underneath in the comment box was a row of red love-hearts.

She tapped on the original post to see who the woman was, but other than the row of hearts, the only other comments were made by him, which was odd – it looked like half the conversation was missing. Caroline tapped on the name of the woman to look at her Facebook page, but whoever she was, her account was private, and the image was a blank avatar. *She must be an ex,* Caroline thought. *Weird how her image is on his feed but there's nothing at all on her page. It must be a fake profile.*

She went back to her messages and read his to her again. Why was she so bothered about it? It was just a message, and if she wanted to, she could simply ignore it. She looked at his image again and thought how he'd helped her yesterday. It was kind of nice, and it wasn't like he'd hung around after she'd put the books in her car – he'd gone straight back into the library. She wondered what books he was taking out, and then began to imagine what genre he read, then decided, *why not?*

Hello Chris. Thank you for your message, slept like a log thanks, always do. Why did she put that? That was too much information, so she deleted it – *Hello Chris, thanks for the message, yes, looks like it's going to be a lovely day. You have a good one too.*

Caroline read it and re-read it, wondering if it was too familiar, and if he could read anything into it. 'You overthink things,' Sam always told her. So before she could change her mind she hit send, then slammed her laptop shut and switched off her phone, this time making sure it was switched off, and settled down to read the papers.

She must have nodded off again, because she woke with a start when she heard a loud knocking on her door. She grabbed her phone to see what the time was, but it was still switched off. She jumped out of bed and wrapped her dressing gown round her, wondering who it could be on a Sunday morning.

'You've forgotten, haven't you?' Sam was standing in the porch holding the leads of two very excited terriers.

'Completely,' said Caroline, 'but come in, it'll take me two minutes to get ready.'

'I tried phoning you,' Sam called after her as she rushed into the bathroom, 'but your phone's off, or broken, or both. You really need to get that sorted you know. You need to be on the end of the phone every minute – you never know what scoop you might be missing.'

'Sorry,' Caroline called from the shower, 'I switched it off in case someone messaged me. I'll tell you about it when I get out.'

As they walked across the park, Caroline explained what had happened the previous day, and told Sam about the message that morning.

Sam found his feed on her phone and scrolled through the first few posts: 'He looks nice, and nothing out of the ordinary here, in fact, it's pretty boring. Maybe he's a bit like you, a techno numpty – he could be your perfect match!'

By the time they walked back it was early afternoon, so they decided to get a pub lunch. They paused at the edge of the road to let a cyclist pass, and it was only when he gave a quick wave and called out 'Morning!' that Caroline realised it was Chris. But by then he had passed and was heading out of the village. 'That was him,' she said to Sam.

'Who?' Sam looked at the receding figure that was kitted out in luminous cycling gear and going at some speed, 'Oh, him? He's a fitness fanatic, too, by the look of those calf muscles. Nothing to dislike about him so far.' She hooked her arm through Caroline's as they walked into the pub.

The following day, Caroline went to the local Starbucks to meet a local researcher, Julie, to help with some missing information. Whilst they waited in the queue, Caroline glanced to the other end of the counter and saw Chris serving someone. He looked up at the exact same moment and gave her an awkward shy wave.

By the time they reached the front of the queue he'd disappeared, perhaps on his break, which Caroline was pleased about; she didn't want him serving her. She led the way to the far side of the room and found a table so she could sit with her back to the counter, and opened her laptop then logged onto the Wi-Fi.

'I hope you don't have anything on there you want to keep secure,' Julie said.

Caroline looked up from her screen. 'What do you mean?'

'The last time I logged onto a public Wi-Fi, within hours my email was hacked, and my social media. It's only because I was changing banks that they didn't get into that too. I use VPN now; it's completely secure.'

'Right – I'm not sure, I'll check it later,' Caroline said, but figured Starbucks wouldn't have anyone infiltrating their system, or everyone would be hacked. Still, she made a mental note to ask her brother.

Later that evening, her phone pinged several times in quick succession, and when she scrolled through the messages from her friends telling her they'd received a 'friend request' from her, she realised her social media *had* been hacked, and when Sam rang her and said she'd just got a really weird email from her, Julie's warning rang in her ears.

So she spent time changing her passwords for everything and checked her bank account, then messaged her brother asking him to sort out a VPN for her.

When she checked her messages later, there was one from Chris that had been sent around the time she found she'd been hacked, and with all the fuss of changing her passwords she hadn't noticed it. *Nice to see you earlier. I wondered if you'd like to go out for a drink some time. Maybe Friday night, around 8?*

She had nothing planned, so why not?

Thank you, that would be great. See you around 8 – no, she thought, *too keen*, and she replaced the '*great*' with '*nice*'. He replied with a thumbs-up.

∞∞

The week flew by, and by Friday evening Caroline could see most of her weekend was going to be taken up with writing the article, already overdue. Then she remembered her date with Chris and began to wish she hadn't agreed to it. But with less than ten minutes to get ready, she gave her hair a quick brush, touched up her morning makeup, and grabbed her phone.

As she headed down to the pub, she started to regret not making a little bit more of an effort, at the very least having a quick shower. But she was late, so she shrugged it off and told herself he'd probably been at Starbucks all day and would smell of paninis and cappuccino. She couldn't have been more wrong.

'Hello, what can I get you?' he asked.

'Half a lager shandy please, and sorry I'm late, deadlines and all that.'

'That's all right. Why not go and grab that table, and I'll bring the drinks over.'

Caroline went over to the small round table in the corner of the room, and noticed it had a 'reserved' sign on it, so she hesitated.

When Chris came over, he pushed the sign aside and said, 'Don't worry, it was for us. I figured it might be busy tonight, so booked ahead.'

Chris turned out to be very interesting; after leaving university, he had travelled across Cambodia and Thailand, then made his way around the Bay of Bengal by boat until he reached India, where he lived in a remote village to help build a schoolhouse, before returning to the UK three years later.

He'd been told there was a job waiting for him in the UK, but it was in accountancy, and after living so long in the village with nothing but the sun and moon to dictate his days, he soon found the job dull. So, when he was offered redundancy five years later, he took it, and had made do with an assortment of jobs ever since whilst he built up an IT business. He was very interested to hear about her work, too, and asked how her research was going.

It was only when the landlord called last orders that Caroline realised they'd been talking for over two hours, and with a planned early start the next day, she knew she'd have to go home soon. After three half-pints, she also needed to visit the ladies, and when she came out, Chris was waiting for her near the door: 'Here's your phone. You left it on the table.'

'Thanks, it's probably switched itself off by now, I really need a new one, I dropped it in the bath.'

'If you want, I could help with that; there are plenty of good deals around,' he said as he handed it back to her.

'Thanks, I'll bear it in mind. Anyway, thanks for a nice evening.'

'Pleasure, I enjoyed it too. Would you like me to walk you home?'

'That's all right, you don't need to. I only live up there, so it's not far.'

'Okay, up to you. I'm down there. Maybe we could do this again sometime.' They were standing outside the pub, and after a relaxed evening, there was now an awkward tension.

'Yes, maybe we could, but I'm full-on busy at the moment, with tight deadlines,' Caroline said, trying to make light of it.

'Okay – let me know when you fancy some time away from your laptop,' he said, and bent down to kiss her on the cheek.

Caroline smiled. 'I will and thank you again for a nice night.'

They each turned and headed in the opposite direction, Caroline pressed the home button on her phone, but it was dead.

∞∞

'I've set your laptop up with a VPN,' said Simon, 'and the only other thing you need to be careful of is NFC.'

Caroline frowned at her brother, who had called round early the next day: 'I wish you wouldn't use acronyms all the time. What *are* you talking about?'

'Near Field Communication. It's when one device can exchange information with another if they're in close proximity to each other.'

'And how do I stop that happening?'

'Keep your phone with you, don't have it in your back pocket or leave it lying around. It takes just a few seconds for someone to transmit the data from your phone to theirs if they know what they're doing.'

'All very James Bond,' Caroline said.

'Not at all,' said Simon. 'It's actually quite simple, unless you're a techno numpty like you. Anyway, it's all done for you now,' and he slid her laptop over the table to her. 'Don't have any more IT problems over the next fortnight. I'm heading off to the wilds of the Orkneys tomorrow.'

'Sounds very remote and desolate, but probably good for the soul. Jess going?'

'It was her idea; she wants to visit Skara Brae, and Maeshowe to see the Viking carvings.'

'That'll be interesting,' she said as he headed for the door. 'Anyway, thanks for that, and when you get back, I need to talk to you about a new phone. This one's definitely had it – it keeps doing odd things.'

'How many times have I heard that?' he said. 'I guarantee you'll still have that phone this time next year.'

'Probably. Have fun with the Vikings.'

The rest of her day was taken up with editing the article – and then, when she arrived for her appointment with the editor on Monday morning, she found the meeting had been postponed to the next day.

'You've got the wrong date. We messaged you this morning. It's tomorrow, midday.' The girl at the desk was an intern and obviously fed up answering the phone and dealing with queries. Caroline checked her phone, but there was nothing there. No point in arguing. Then just as she was walking out of the building her phone pinged, and there was the message. She looked at its sent time – three hours earlier, at seven thirty that morning. She really was going to have to get a new phone.

Rather than go straight home, she decided to go to the café next door. She sat in the bay window that overlooked the busy high street and was surprised to see Chris walking into the shop opposite. A few minutes later he came back out and looked up and down the high street as if he was searching for someone. She was in two minds whether to invite him to join her but decided not. She wondered who he might be meeting.

A couple of days later her phone pinged, and it was a message from Chris: '*Hope the editor liked the article. Let me know if you'd like to meet up again, I'd like to see you again, if you want to.*'

Caroline smiled. It was quite nice getting the attention, but she was happy to keep it casual for the time being, so she put her phone to one side – he was going to have to wait for her reply.

Later that evening she wrote: *Yes she did. And yes, that'd be nice. I'm flat out at the moment, though, so maybe towards the end of the week.*

She then went through the images on her phone, deleting the ones she didn't want and plugged it into the charger.

∞∞

'Would you like a garlic bread to share?' the waiter asked.

Caroline and Chris were sitting in the pub on the Friday night. It had been very last-minute; she'd realised she didn't have any food for the weekend and couldn't be bothered to go shopping, so when Chris had contacted her again and asked if she fancied meeting up that evening, she'd figured *why not*?

'Okay, thanks, and I'll have the pasta please, but no olives,' she said as she handed the menu back to the waiter, who headed to the kitchen with their order.

'How'd the meeting go with the editor? All sorted?' Chris asked.

'Yep, all sorted,' Caroline replied, 'though it was annoying to get there on Monday morning to find they'd rescheduled the appointment. My stupid phone didn't receive the message until it was too late.'

Chris laughed. 'You really *do* need a new phone, or one day you'll miss that offer of a million-pound book deal.'

'I know! It seems to have a mind of its own now. I deleted a load of images the other night, but the next morning they were all still there. It's such a hassle. When my brother gets back, I'll ask him to sort it out for me.'

'You know I'd be happy to help if you wanted. I know a thing or two about them – the best deals, what's worth it and what isn't. But only if you want. I have to go to Norwich tomorrow to get a new laptop, so if you want, I could pick you up on my way through, and help with finding the right phone for you.'

'That's all right, I'm not sure what I want anyway, so I'll leave it a bit longer,' she replied, sipping her wine. 'Anyway, I was going to say I saw you, when I went for a coffee after my not-meeting.'

'Oh? Not spying on me, I hope.' Chris said, grinning.

'Yeah, no. Funny though, what were the chances of me being there for an appointment that didn't happen, and going for a coffee just at the moment you go to the shop opposite?'

'Quite,' he said. 'What were the chances? Maybe kismet was at work that day.'

Caroline was starting to enjoy being with Chris. They got on well, seemed to have similar interests, and having thought earlier that she'd be eating nothing more than cheesy chips for dinner, it was turning out to be a nice evening. When the landlord called last orders and Chris offered to walk her home, she happily agreed.

'Thank you for a lovely evening,' she said.

'My pleasure, and if you change your mind about tomorrow, message me, I won't be leaving until mid-morning.'

'Okay, thanks.' Caroline closed her front door and made her way into the lounge feeling quite pleased with everything when her phone pinged,

Just heading back from the surgery, wondered if you fancied fish & chips over at mine The message was from Sam, and although it had been sent a few minutes before she'd got Chris's message inviting her to dinner that evening it had only just appeared on her phone. She tapped in her reply, *Sorry, stupid phone has only just sent this to me!*

Sam's reply came back within seconds, *You really do need to get a new phone! No worries, I'm off out with the boys tomorrow afternoon if you need to stretch your legs*

Before she replied to Sam, Caroline tapped in a message to Chris: *Just missed another message, I think maybe I should get a new phone sorted after all, so if it's no bother I'll go with you tomorrow*

Within seconds his reply came back, *No problem at all. Pick you up around 10.30*

Caroline replied with a thumbs-up then messaged Sam to say she'd head over around two thirty the next day.

Later that night, rather than switching her phone off as usual, she plugged it in and left it switched on to make sure she wouldn't miss another message, then put it face down, putting it on mute. That meant she didn't see it light up when the new-message notification flashed up, nor did she see the message, from Simon, being deleted.

∞∞

Chris arrived just before ten thirty the next day. 'Have you checked your phone for messages?' he asked as she got into his car. 'I wouldn't want you to miss that all-important one.'

'Ha ha, very funny, and yes, I have. There've been none since my reply to Sam last night. Though I was expecting one from my brother – odd, that, as he usually does when he goes away.'

'Perhaps the signal's bad up there; it may arrive later today. Anyway, I've had a quick search for the kind of phone I think'd suit you, which will hopefully narrow it down a bit for you.'

Caroline smiled, it was nice to have someone thinking about this stuff so she didn't have to, although she didn't want him to think she was incapable of thinking for herself. 'Great, thanks, though I have a rough idea of what I want, and it's going to be down to cost at the end of the day.'

'Of course. I'm sure we'll find something to suit,' he said as he pulled off and headed toward the main road out of the village.

It was less than thirty minutes' drive, and it passed very quickly as they chatted about their favourite music, books, films – all the things people talk about when they're getting to know one another. It was uncanny how similar they were, and Chris' taste in music was as eclectic as hers.

After they had parked up, Chris checked his phone. 'Sorry, I have a couple of messages I need to respond to. It won't take a minute.'

'Sure, no problem. I'm just going to take a look in that bookshop over there whilst you do.'

Caroline was scanning the rows of second-hand books when her phone pinged with a message notification. It was from Simon, and was surprisingly brief – he usually relayed some kind of story about his journey and always with a picture, but this time it was a simple: *enroute but signal awful so will message when I can*

Caroline tapped in a reply then carried on looking along the shelves when Chris joined her. 'Find what you're looking for?' he asked.

'Not really, I was just browsing. Simon's message has just come through. He said the signal was bad. Not like him, though, he usually finds a way. Anyway, shall we go find the best deal for me?'

∞∞

It was surprisingly straightforward and, with just three phones to choose from after Chris had helped her narrow them down, she went for a Samsung Galaxy.

'Well, that was pretty painless. If you want, if you let me have your old phone, I can set the new one up for you,' Chris offered.

'Okay, thanks. I don't want anything complicated. Just the same as what I have now is fine,' Caroline replied as she went to pay for it, leaving the phones with Chris.

As they drove back, Caroline checked everything that she needed was on the new phone. 'Thanks for helping out with this, and no offence, but I'll change the password to get into it.'

Chris laughed, 'None taken, and it's a good idea. You should really change your passwords regularly to keep everything secure.'

'That's what Simon tells me, and I always mean to but it just never happens. Anyway, at least I have a phone now that will hopefully stop losing messages in the ether.'

The rest of the weekend was taken up with more research, writing up notes and catching up with Sam. 'It's nice,' Caroline told her. 'It's like he understands me, there's no pressure, no urgent messages or anything. He's happy to let it roll – and before you ask, no we haven't.'

Sam raised her eyebrows in disbelief. 'Glad to hear it, and how's the new phone?'

'It's ideal. No more missed messages or the battery dying within minutes, and it takes great pictures.' Caroline held it up and took a picture of Sam to show her.

A few days later, Sam messaged her: *Met him today. I'm not surprised you like him, what a charmer. He said he recognised me from your description*

Caroline smiled, and was about to reply when she realised she couldn't recall telling Chris about Sam, or at least not what she looked like. But maybe she'd mentioned something in passing.

The following day when she switched her phone on, it immediately pinged telling her there was a message from Chris: *Sorry for the radio silence these past few days, it's been really busy for me. Hope the phone is working OK*

Caroline noticed it had been sent at three in the morning and felt quite sorry for him. If he was so busy that was tough, she felt, and she replied straight away, which was most unlike her: *No problem, I've been up to my neck too. Phone is perfect thanks.*

Within seconds his reply came back. *Glad to hear it. If you're not busy at the weekend, would you like to go and see Double Indemnity? It's showing at the Picture House. But if that's not your thing, don't worry.*

This came as a bit of a surprise to Caroline – she hadn't expected anyone she knew to know about that film, let alone want to see it: *I was planning to see that, thanks, I'd like that*

He answered straight away. *Perfect, pick you up around 7 on Sat night x*

Caroline smiled, that was the first time he'd finished with an 'x', *and* he wanted to take her to see a film that she never imagined anyone would have heard about. When she'd searched for screenings and seen the Picture House was showing it, she'd wanted to go but hadn't got round to booking a ticket. She replied, *Thank you, see you then x*

∞∞

On the Saturday morning she did a quick online click-and-collect food shop, including a couple of bags of her favourite snacks to take to the film. So when Chris picked her up later and passed her a bag saying there were some snacks for them in there, and she opened it to see the same flavour bag of popcorn and sweets, she said, 'You have to be kidding,' as she took hers from her bag. 'That's just too weird! What were the chances of you buying the exact same thing?'

Chris laughed and put them back in his bag. 'Well in that case we'll have yours and I'll keep mine for later.'

The film was excellent, and it was only as the closing credits were rolling and Chris turned to her to ask if she had enjoyed it, that he leant over and kissed her. It was the most exquisite moment she had felt in a long time.

The next day she was expecting to see a message from him, but there was nothing, so she messaged him. *Thank you for a lovely evening, I enjoyed it very much x*

She expected an immediate reply as usual, but there was nothing. She kept checking her phone, but it was a couple of hours later before he replied. *Yes, it was a great film, glad you enjoyed it. Enjoy the rest of your day x*

By the afternoon, having sat at her laptop the whole time, Caroline needed a walk, and she was just about to cross the road when she had to wait for a stream of cyclists to pass. She didn't pay much attention to them until the last few. One of them slowed down and she realised it was Chris. He waved but carried on. She looked after him and felt just a bit disappointed he hadn't at least stopped to say hello. She checked her phone for messages and walked on down the path.

It was a couple of days later that she was in the supermarket when she saw him in the wine aisle. She stood next to him and said, 'The Merlot would be my choice.'

He did a double-take and then smiled. 'Well, hello. Are you sure you're not following me? First the bike race and now in the supermarket.'

'Ha ha, I'd make a terrible spy,' Caroline replied, smiling. 'I'm far too obvious, and rubbish at keeping secrets.'

'Me too,' Chris replied. 'You off out tonight?'

'Just over to Sam's – well, hopefully,' she replied.

'Why 'hopefully'? Has something happened?' Chris asked.

'Not sure. She said she was feeling a bit unwell.'

'Sorry to hear that, I hope it's nothing serious. Anyway, enjoy the rest of your week.'

'Thanks, you too.' She smiled to herself as she grabbed the few bits she needed for the evening at Sam's.

Later, as she was unpacking the bags on her kitchen table, her phone pinged, it was a message from Sam. *Really sorry, we're going to have to postpone tonight. I feel awful, not sure what it is, but probably best you don't come over just in case*

Caroline replied straight away. *Poor you. Let me know if you need anything, hopefully it's just a 24-hour thing, maybe something you ate. Call you tomorrow*

Sam replied with a thumbs-up, and Caroline carried on unpacking the food bags. It was just a few minutes later her phone pinged again. She thought it might be Sam asking for something, so she read the message straight away: *You were right, the Merlot is very good. If you end up not going to Sam's, why not join me?*

Caroline stared at her phone, *that's a coincidence,* she thought, *how odd he should message so soon after Sam.* She tapped in her reply. *Thanks, but I think I'll stay in tonight, enjoy the Merlot*

Then she tapped the screen again to play some music and noticed the battery was nearly dead – which was odd, too, because it had been fully charged that morning and she hadn't used it that much.

∞∞

The next day, Caroline decided to go for a swim. She had got out of the habit of regular exercise, so it felt good to really push herself, and after twenty lengths her arms and legs were starting to ache.

It was nearly midday by the time she had finished, so she messaged Sam to see how she was feeling, and said she'd drop in on her way home. She noticed the battery was only half-charged again, which made no sense because it had been fully charged that morning and all she'd done was search for the opening times of the pool, send a few messages, and make two phone calls.

She headed out of the changing rooms, stopping by the vending machine to buy a snack.

'We really must stop meeting like this.'

She spun around and came face to face with Chris. 'Oh, hello. What are you doing here?'

'I belong to the gym. You've been swimming by the looks of things.'

'Yes, I decided I needed to get back to some form of exercise. I've been so busy I haven't done anything for months.'

'Well don't go spoiling it by eating chocolate.' His tone had a condescending edge to it. 'Anyway, I'm heading home now, to finish that bottle of Merlot. You can join me if you want.'

'Thanks, maybe later. I said I'd drop in to see Sam. Thankfully she's better now, so it was most likely something she ate.'

Disappointment fell across his face. 'That's a pity – that you can't, I mean, not that Sam's better, obviously that's good news she's better.'

'Yes, well anyway, it's nice seeing you again,' she said as she swung her bag over her shoulder. 'Enjoy the Merlot. I'd better get a move on, lots to do.'

'Thanks, you have a good one too,' Chris said as he watched her walk out to her car.

She dropped her phone into the hands-free holder in her car when it pinged: a message from her brother. *Anyone there?*

She replied straight away. *About time. How's it going? I was beginning to think you'd disappeared down a dark Viking hole*

His reply came back almost immediately. *That's rich. Been messaging you loads, you NEED to get your phone sorted! Anyway, we're staying on another week.*

That *was* odd. Caroline replied saying she'd message him later, then scrolled back through the thread. The last message from her brother was four days ago.

When she was sitting in Sam's comfy living room later, it turned out that there were several of Sam's messages missing too.

'Maybe there's something wrong with the phone,' Sam suggested, 'and if the battery's running out too quickly as well, I'd say there's definitely something wrong. Take it back to the shop and ask for an exchange or your money back.'

'I will. There's obviously something wrong with it. Anyway, how are you? What do you think it was?' Caroline asked Sam.

'The only thing I ate was a sandwich I bought from Starbucks. I don't usually get anything from them, but I was running late and happened to be driving past. I meant to tell you, I saw Chris in there, and he ended up serving me.'

'Oh? Odd he didn't tell me,' Caroline replied.

∞∞

The next day Caroline went into Norwich and took her phone back to the shop. She hadn't mentioned anything to Chris because she was beginning to feel something wasn't right.

The techie checked the phone, then said, 'It's your GPS that's draining the battery. If you're in an area with a good signal, it'll use around 13 per cent, but go to somewhere with a weak signal and you're looking at 38 per cent or more drain with the tracking on.'

Caroline was standing in the brightly lit phone shop, watching him as he scrolled, double- and triple-tapped the screen of her new phone with the ease that was second nature to Gen Z. She looked at him blankly: 'I don't know what you mean. What tracking?'

'Your GPS tracking's on, and it looks like your phone's linked to Minspy as well, which means your exact location can be tracked, and it can also tell where you've been, and monitor your email, social media, and messages.'

'Can you remove it, and make it secure so that can't happen again?'

'Sure, we can do a factory reset. You just need to back up all your data, then the reset will remove everything.'

There was only one person who could have done those things, and faced with this knowledge she knew what she had to do. 'That's all right. There's nothing on there I want to keep, so you can do the factory reset now.'

'Sure? No photos or messages you want to check first?'

'No, nothing I want to keep. Go ahead and reset it.' What he'd told her was the final part of a puzzle she'd been trying to work out, and now she had the full picture she was certain she'd made the right decision.

When she got home, she blocked Chris's phone number, and blocked him on her social media platforms as well. It felt liberating. Now he wouldn't be able to contact her or find out what she was doing without her knowledge, and she'd already planned in her head what she was going to say if she came face to face with him.

∞∞

Don't forget to put your bananas facing up to show you're single. And if you fancy someone, put a peach in their trolley

Caroline read Sam's message and replied with a laugh. After Sam's attempt to get her to join online dating, Caroline was holding off following any more of the advice Sam had picked up from the magazines in her waiting room. Now, having managed to avoid seeing

Chris for the past few days, so not needing to say what she'd planned about the phone having to be reset by the shop because of a virus – nor that she'd been too busy to catch up with him, and that she hoped all was well, and that she would see him around (which meant she would absolutely *not* be seeing him again) – she was happy to stay single for the time being, *and* in control of who she let into her life.

But having avoided the supermarket for several days, and managing on what was left in the freezer, Caroline found herself in the place she detested more than most. What was it about the weekly food shop she hated? Maybe it was because at best she did it fortnightly, which meant when she went to the Basket Only checkout with an overflowing basket and several more items tucked under her arm, not only was she scowled at by other shoppers, but also it meant she never had enough bags to put everything in – which was why it turned out that someone had been following her across the car park.

'I think you may need these later.'

She'd been concentrating on trying to make space in the boot of her car, pushing all the clobber in it to the back, and hadn't noticed anyone following her, let alone standing next to her, so momentarily she wondered why someone was standing there with a twelve-pack of toilet roll, until she noticed hers was missing. 'Oops, didn't realise I'd left those behind, thank you.'

'No problem – though I'm not sure you're going to get anything else in there,' he said nodding at the full car boot.

With another bag at her feet, Caroline had to agree with him, 'I think you're right. There's still the passenger seat.'

She pulled the lid of the boot down, and just as she did, the bag by her feet fell over and two oranges started to roll away. He laughed as he picked them up. 'Tell you what, you open your car door and I'll pass this to you.'

'And this is why I hate food shopping,' Caroline said with a half-smile as she moved round to the side of her car to put the bag in the footwell. 'Thanks. Sorry about that.'

'Like I say, no problem. I know what you mean, though, and Saturdays are the worst. You could always try online shopping.'

'I did once and ended up with several bags of bananas and no toilet roll!'

They both laughed as she wedged the bag behind the seat. 'Thanks again,' she said.

'You're welcome. And it's Mike,' he said, smiling.

'Thank you, Mike, I'm Caroline.'

'Have a good day, Caroline,' he said as he turned and walked away, and just as she was shutting her car door, she smiled to herself when she noticed the bunch of bananas poking out of the top of her bag.

∞∞

Why Caroline had agreed to it, she wasn't sure, and as she walked into the pub, she was even more certain it was a mistake. Maybe it wasn't too late to message Laura that she'd got a migraine and couldn't make it. But it *was* too late; the moment she'd walked through the door her friend waved at her and came over to greet her.

'I'm really not sure about this, Laura,' said Caroline. 'A blind date's so embarrassing.

'Rubbish!' said Laura. 'He's really nice and a bit like you, isn't long out of a bad relationship, and if it doesn't work out, then you've lost nothing – but if you don't give it a go you'll never know.'

They walked back to the table and Caroline was surprised to see Mike sitting there. 'Oh, hello again,' she said as Mike stood up.

Laura looked from one to the other. 'You know each other?'

'Not exactly,' Caroline said. 'Mike rescued my oranges from certain death in the supermarket car park a couple of weeks ago.'

'Well, that's even better, I don't need to do the introductions,' Laura said.

'Not so sure it makes it any less awkward,' Caroline replied.

'Yes – sorry about my cousin,' Mike said. 'She means well. Anyway, let me get you a drink.'

'Thanks, I'll have half a lager shandy.'

Caroline sat down as Mike went over to the bar.

'I've told him all about you,' said Laura.

'Hopefully not,' Caroline said. 'That's enough to put anyone off.'

'Don't be silly! You're both single, and both have busy working lives, which means you never get out and meet people. I'm sure you'll get on.'

'He's good-looking, and you've told me he's a firefighter. I'm sure he doesn't need any help.'

'He's a bit bruised after his last relationship,' Laura replied, ignoring Caroline's comment. 'She was very possessive and turned out to have a few issues, and he vowed to stay single after that. But that was weeks ago. Anyway, stay for just one drink at least.'

The evening turned out to be very pleasant, and whilst Caroline and Mike didn't make any firm arrangement, they did exchange phone numbers. And a couple of days later he sent a message to see if she wanted to meet up, but this time without his cousin.

Over dinner, Mike explained the problem he'd had with Stacey, his girlfriend, after they'd split up, and whilst Caroline didn't push him to tell her anything, he was happy to share his story.

They hadn't known each other long, four months at most, but within a fortnight of knowing each other she'd become obsessed with him, never wanting to leave his side, and when they were apart she would message him constantly, becoming increasingly agitated when he didn't respond straight away. Evenings out having fun soon became evenings in, and if he wanted to go somewhere without her, she'd accuse him of seeing someone else. She obviously had anxiety issues, and after losing her job as a teacher's assistant, she worked part-time for a holiday letting agency. That was okay – but then, when she started leaving her belongings in his flat, rearranging his furniture and finally asking for her own key, he decided he had to finish it.

In the days and weeks that followed, it became obvious she was not going to accept their break-up.

It was easy enough to stop her calling him – he simply blocked her number and the same on social media, so she had no means of direct contact with him; but she would still turn up at places he went to, and started monitoring his friends' social media to see if she could find out what he was doing and who he was with. She would turn up at his workplace with gifts and leave messages on his car windscreen or post them through his door.

In the end he closed all his social media accounts, and changed his phone number, which seemed to help. But a short time later his station had a call-out to a small house fire at her address. 'I wasn't there at the time,' Mike said, 'it was my day off, but they said when they arrived, it soon became obvious it had been started deliberately. She was lucky no one was hurt, and when she was told I wasn't part of the crew, she completely broke down.'

Mike went on to say she'd received a suspended sentence on condition she had counselling. All of that had left him feeling reluctant to get involved with someone again.

Caroline was sympathetic, and told Mike about her experience with Chris, which seemed quite tame by comparison, and they both agreed it was unnerving to think someone was able to monitor your every move without you knowing.

'It's one of the drawbacks of twenty-first-century life,' Caroline said. 'Everyone knows what everyone else is doing – it's become second nature to publish your most personal information. We're all guilty of it in one form or another, each of us trying to find out what others are doing. Either comparing our life with theirs or living their life vicariously through them. It's so easy now to find out most things about anyone. But the drawback, as I found out, is not knowing if the person who's following you on social media is quite literally following you.'

'But it must be an essential part of your job,' said Mike, 'being on social media, keeping people in the loop of your life all the time. But it must feel like you're permanently on display, with everyone knowing your business. Laura told me it's sometimes a job to keep up with you, though she did tell me you're planning to go away soon.'

'Yes, I am. I've planned a weekend break not far from here – just needed a change of scene for a couple of days – though I have to admit I got my dates mixed up. It's not this weekend but next. Funnily enough, I found out from the holiday firm I'd tagged in my post about it; they messaged me in a panic telling me my booking's for next week. I was going to add a comment to my post, but I haven't got round to it. I'll maybe make a joke about it next week, something about the writer who never writes things down. Anyway, chances are that other than Laura no one took any notice, and even if they did, today's post is tomorrow's fish and chip wrapper. People forget very easily and quickly.'

They got on well together and were easy in each other's company, like old friends catching up, but there was no spark. So, when Mike told Caroline he had put in for a transfer to another station, and would be moving to Bristol at the weekend, she wasn't particularly disappointed, and said she hoped it'd be a fresh start for him.

∞∞

On the Friday before Mike's move, the local florist delivered a small bouquet to Caroline. There was no card, and when she asked the florist who the flowers had come from, she said it had been an internet order and didn't know. The only person Caroline could think of was Mike, so she sent him a text wishing him luck with the move and thanks for the flowers.

He replied straight away, saying the flowers were not from him. Perhaps, then, they were from Chris, she thought – but he'd have no reason to be so mysterious about his identity, surely?

But with a looming deadline, she was too busy to worry about it. She wanted to get the final draft finished before the weekend, and it was already midday. She was grateful that at least she didn't have to think about packing for the weekend.

It was only when her phone pinged several hours later that she realised how late it was, and whilst she had finished the article and was happy with it, the message that appeared on her phone made her feel anything but. *Lucky you got your dates wrong, looks like your weekend away just went up in smoke*

The message was from Sam, and she had attached a link to a news report:

Holiday home destroyed in fire

Fire crews were called to the property in Stallyridge at 2am today after reports of a house fire. 'I was driving past when I saw the smoke, and called the emergency services, but by the time they arrived the fire had taken hold,' said passer-by Chris Saunders, who had been on his way to a late-night shift.

Incident Commander Ian Lance said: 'When our crews arrived, they were faced with an end-terrace house that was completely alight. The roof quickly collapsed, and our concern was that the fire would spread to adjoining properties. Our crews did a fantastic job of surrounding the fire both from the ground and above, and bringing it under control quickly. It's incredible the fire hasn't spread, and it's thanks to the firefighters' skill and hard work that we're not looking at multiple houses involved in this fire.'

At 2.30am Cadent arrived and turned off the gas. Then the crews extinguished the final flames, which had been fed by a small gas leak. The firefighters have spent the morning at the incident damping down the area and making sure it is safe. There has been significant fire damage to the property and the property has been left uninhabitable.

There is one victim, whose body has not yet been identified. The cause of the fire is undetermined, and a full investigation will take place once it is safe to do so. Police are asking anyone with CCTV or video footage that might help with their investigations to get in touch.

Caroline tried to find more news about it, but there was nothing. She ran a search for *fire Stallyridge* across all her social media, but there was just one post, put up by the local paper, which linked back to the same article. Then she did a search under Chris's name, but because she'd blocked him, she couldn't even see his profile, and if she removed the block, it would be forty-eight hours before she could ask to be friends with him again. And even then, the chances were he'd ignore her request, which would be even more frustrating.

So she phoned Sam to see if she could see anything on *her* timeline. Whilst Sam could see Chris's profile, he'd changed his privacy settings so she could no longer see any of his posts, and there were no other posts he'd been tagged in linking him to the fire.

'If there's an investigation because someone's died,' Sam told Caroline, 'they've probably stopped anything being posted. They have to establish whether or not it was accidental.'

'But why was Chris there at that time? Seems a bit of a coincidence – and who died in the fire?' asked Caroline.

'Who knows?' said Sam. 'But it's quite scary to think that it could have been you.'

'I hadn't thought of *that*,' said Caroline, shuddering. They both tried to find more information, but there was nothing other than the one report.

Caroline didn't sleep much that night, and when she woke early the next day, she immediately ran a search for updates. There was another report, but it only served to raise yet more questions in her mind:

> Local florist Danni's Flowers tell us they had been asked to deliver a bouquet to the address, which they did at around 5pm on Thursday. The cleaner doing the changeover said she would put the flowers in a vase for the guest arriving on Friday.
>
> The neighbouring house CCTV showed Chris Saunders' car pulling up outside the property just after 6pm, and he was seen walking to the back of the holiday house, returning to his car ten minutes later. He appeared to be alone.
>
> No one else was seen entering or leaving the house. At 2am Saunders was driving past and said he saw the smoke coming from the upstairs window, which was when he called the emergency services.
>
> The body of the victim has been identified as local resident Stacey Roberts. The police confirmed an autopsy will be carried out to establish the cause of death. Her family are being supported by specialist officers and they have asked for privacy at this tragic time.

Chris Saunders is helping the police with their inquiries, but no charges have been brought.

What the hell? thought Caroline, *Talk about six degrees of separation!* She typed *Stacey Roberts* into the search bar; there were nearly three pages of news reports, all of them giving a similar story. It was too big a coincidence – it had to be the same Stacey Roberts that Mike knew, and Caroline wondered if she should message Mike – if he was staying away from social media, maybe he hadn't seen it. So she typed, *Not sure if you've seen the news, hope things are OK*

She leant against her kitchen counter, staring out of the window, hugging a cup of steaming coffee, trying to make sense of events, and nearly jumped out of her skin when the doorbell rang.

When she opened the door, she was surprised to see someone with a bouquet of flowers: 'You're a popular person.' It was the courier who had delivered the last bunch.

Caroline didn't feel like smiling. Ordinarily she loved receiving flowers, but after everything that had happened, she'd never wanted flowers less than she did now. But she smiled and said, 'I guess so – two bouquets in two days! Just wish I knew who was sending them, unless there's a card this time.'

'There is – though it doesn't say who they're from, either I'm afraid,' said the woman, 'and it's not your second, it's your *third*. The second was the large bouquet for you that we delivered to that Stallyridge house, the one that burnt down. What a terrible thing that was! Must've been a shock for you.'

Caroline knew when to keep her mouth shut. 'Yes,' she said to the woman, 'tragic – but thank you for these, they're lovely.' Taking the flowers, she closed the door. *Who's sending the flowers? And has the same person sent all three?* she asked herself. *Whoever it is, someone knows I was planning to stay at the Stallyridge house.*

She put the flowers on the side, flipped open her laptop and logged onto her Facebook account, pulling up her previous posts. She scrolled down, looking at each one from the last two weeks; Stacey Roberts had liked them all. She had been following Caroline's every move, which meant she would have known Caroline was going to stay at the holiday let – but she wouldn't have known that Caroline had got the date wrong.

Caroline tapped on the list to see who else had liked the same post as Stacey; there was a tall column of different emojis; over a hundred people had reacted to the post about her weekend away in Stallyridge. Some of the names she vaguely recognised, but most of them she didn't.

Then Caroline put Stacey's name in the search bar and found to her surprise that the account was a public one. When Caroline tapped on her recent posts to see who had interacted with them, she saw Chris's name appear on the last few entries.

∞∞

Caroline drew up a timeline, starting with her first post Stacey had liked. It coincided with the time she had met Mike at the pub with Laura.

Then she scrolled through Stacey's own feed to see when Chris had started to follow her posts. Just over a week ago.

She looked over at the bouquet of flowers she had put on the side, reached over, and pulled off the small envelope, removing the card that was inside. The anonymous message read *Sorry about the fire, I hope you still get your break.*

"The trick to following someone without getting caught is to follow somebody who doesn't think they're being followed."

Lemony Snicket

CASE STUDY

This is Melissa's story. Her name has been changed, but that is all, and what happened to her may be happening to you, or someone you know. It's not that uncommon.

Melissa's phone was bought for her by her partner; nothing unusual in that, and sometimes it makes good business sense, or that's what we're told.

Q. You didn't buy your own phone?

A. No. My husband bought it. It made sense - everything went through the company books; I didn't really think about it. Each month the bill was paid by the company too, and he had an itemised bill from the phone provider that showed every call I made, each text message I sent, everything. But I didn't know that, like I say, I didn't really think about it. I mean, you wouldn't, would you?

Q. You subsequently found out he had been monitoring your calls.

A. Yes, he would get an itemised bill that showed every message, phone call, all the contacts I made on my phone.

Q. Then you discovered he had put a tracker on your car.

A. The tracker had been fitted when he bought the car for me, but for three years, I had no idea he was tracking every journey I made. I remember one evening I had been at a flower arranging course with his mum, and when I got back, he said, *'who have you been shagging?'* He knew I'd been with his mum but accused me of stopping off to see someone on my way home.

Q. Had he always been this controlling?

A. Looking back, yes, but at the time I didn't realise it. I hated confrontation, would always compromise, back down.

Q. How did it manifest itself?

A. He would do it by stealth. If he didn't like what I was wearing for instance, he would say something like *that colour doesn't suit you,* and I would look at myself and think maybe he was right, and I would change what I was wearing. My wardrobe completely changed over the years, it wasn't *me,* it was *his* version of me.

Q. What else did he say about the way you looked?

A. He told me hooped earrings made me look like a slut. I loved wearing them but stopped when he said that.

Q. What about friends and family, did you turn to them for advice?

A. We lived in a rural setting, so it was quite isolated, and he slowly started to cut me off from everyone. He would say things like *'you don't really want to go to yoga, don't go, I'll miss you',* or *'do you really need to go out with them? It's cold and dark, stay here with me'.*

Q. Was it always like this? What about before you were married?

A. At the time, I didn't notice it, if he did say something, he would make light of it, turn it into a joke, so by the morning it was forgotten about. I'd brush it under the carpet.

Q. If you had your doubts, why did you get married?

A. I thought it would be alright, I suppose the doubts weren't big enough then. I wanted the financial security, the easy life, I figured he wasn't that bad. I remember his dad said something to me the night before the wedding, that at the time seemed odd, but now I understand; he said, *'you don't have to go through with this.'* But I couldn't not go through with it, everyone had arrived to enjoy my big day. But to be honest, deep down, I knew then it wouldn't last.

Q. What about his family? How have they been?

A. His dad has been incredibly supportive; he wasn't surprised when I told him about the tracker on the car. But his mum doesn't accept any of it.

Q. You started a family two years after your marriage, did that change things?

A. Yes. I was in hospital for several weeks with the twins, my husband didn't spend much time with us, so I had plenty of thinking time, and when I talked to the nurses, they made me question the things he did. Then in 2014, my suspicions were raised even more because he would mention something that I had done or said that he would have no way of knowing unless he was following my every move.

Q. Is that why you bought your own phone?

A. Yes. But he soon worked out what I was doing because I was using my normal phone less often.

Q. What was his reaction?

A. He confronted me, told me he knew I had another phone. He turned the house upside down looking for it. I was scared shitless. He eventually found it and destroyed it, but all it did was to raise his suspicions of me even more. He just kept on, *who was I seeing? Where was I going?* I just shut down, I'm not very brave. I would cry a lot, say nothing back.

Q. Couldn't you leave?

A. I wasn't strong enough. I wanted him to hit me, I even asked him to hit me, then people could see what was happening, but because it was verbal, nobody saw that.

Q. But you stayed?

A. Yes. He told me if I left him, I would get nothing from him. That was one of his top trumps. I was terrified at this point. After everything had calmed down, I simply accepted the new phone he bought me.

Q. Did you ever confront him? Ask him why he was doing this to you?

A. Sometimes. He didn't see anything wrong in it, he would say, *'It's just words, I don't know what your problem is'*.

Q. What happened in 2014? What changed everything?

A. I was having panic attacks, I was depressed, felt like I was in a hole. He said I had postnatal depression; I probably did. The twins were about a year old by then.

Q. Did you seek help?

A. I went for counselling. I told them everything. That's when it all changed, when they said, *'You do know this emotional abuse?'* I didn't, it hadn't occurred to me.

Q. But you returned to the family home?

A. Yes, but I was scared, so I started to put things in place, started to set up a new life for me in secret, and when I faced yet another argument, I rang a close friend who told me to pack my bag and leave that night.

Q. What about the children? Did you have somewhere to go?

A. Unbeknown to my husband, I had organised somewhere else for me to live, so I went there with the twins. I'm not sure, if I hadn't had that house, if my friend hadn't told me to pack a bag and leave, I'm not sure I would have had the guts to move out. I think I'd have bottled out.

Q. It's been seven years since you walked out. What's happened in that time?

A. I'm who I used to be. I have a job I thoroughly enjoy, and I have my self-esteem back. I have my life back.

Q. What about your relationship with your ex-husband?

A. He hasn't changed. I have learned how to deal with him, how to avoid a confrontation. He has said he is going to tell the twins what he thinks of me when they are old enough to understand. But by then, I hope they will have learned how manipulative and controlling he is, and they will see him for what he is.

ABOUT THE AUTHOR

Sophia Moseley is an established feature writer for magazines, and children's author; *Unseen Follower* is her latest short story for adults.

Living near the Pearl of Dorset, having spent most of her working life in the City, then joining the Arts & Culture industry, Sophia has written for both local and national magazines, including Liverpool's Lifestyle Monthly, Nursery Education Plus, Woman's Weekly and Dorset Magazine. From chatting to Duncan Bannatyne to researching into historic houses, Sophia has interviewed celebrities and been privy to private collections.

Sophia has also written biographies for private clients and run creative writing workshops in both primary and secondary schools.

Sophia is a Member of the Society of Authors and Authors' Licensing and Collecting Society.

Brindle Books Ltd

We hope that you have enjoyed this book. To find out more about Brindle Books Ltd, including news of new releases, please visit our website:

http://www.brindlebooks.co.uk

There is a contact page on the website, should you have any queries, and you can let us know if you would like email updates of news and new releases. We promise that we won't spam you with lots of sales emails, and we will never sell or give your contact details to any third party.

If you purchased this book online, please consider leaving an honest review on the site from which you purchased it. Your feedback is important to us, and may influence future releases from our company.

To view our current releases, please scan the QR code below:

Other Titles Available from Brindle Books Ltd

MY TIME AGAIN

BY

SOPHIA MOSELEY

Everyone turned to look at Kathy as she walked slowly past. She knew in her heart it was wrong. Her head screamed "No", but she went ahead anyway.

Have you ever wished you could undo a decision you've made? Return to that crossroad in your past and take a different path instead. What alternative life might have awaited you? And what of those you now know and love? Change what has been, and they might never exist at all.

Fate, which you cannot control, predetermines all events. Yet, your destiny is in your hands. Or is it? Which one is the dominant force?

THE 'LOST' VILLAGE OF LAWERS

BY

MARK BRIDGEMAN

The Lost Village of Lawers tells the story of the haunting and enigmatic abandoned village that nestles besides the shores of Loch Tay. Almost 1,000 years of surprising human history are hidden within its tumbling ruins. Unknown, unseen, and forgotten by many, this new publication reveals the story behind the ruins and attempts to answer the question that has puzzled so many people – just who was its most famous resident – 'The Lady of Lawers'?

ERASED:

Missing Persons Mysteries From Around The World

BY

MARK BRIDGEMAN

Every year, millions of people go missing around the world. Over 500,000 in the US and more than 170,000 in the UK alone. Roughly one a minute. Many cases are resolved, some over an agonising period of time. Others, never.

Erased deals with seven of the most mysterious, unfathomable, enigmatic, and little-known cases in history. From the streets of London to the jungles of South America, journey with true crime writer Mark Bridgeman (author of the best-selling 'Perthshire's Pound of Flesh' and 'The Nearly Man') into a world of unanswered questions, unseen perils, and unspoken family secrets.

What really became of the missing millionaire, the Hollywood actress, the missing hiker, or the real Indiana Jones? Is the answer out there somewhere, or are they Erased forever?

TO THE DOURO

By

DAVID J BLACKMORE

A young man's decision to fight leads to a war within a war…

To love…

To loss…

…and a quest for vengeance, as he plays a vital role for the future Duke of Wellington.

The first thrilling adventure in David J Blackmore's WELLINGTON'S DRAGOON series.

NORMANBY

By

P. G. DIXON

Pawns were made to be sacrificed.

When Tom Grant is transferred from the glamour of MI5 to a little-known intelligence department, he begins to think that his career is on the slide.

Then, the investigation into the death of an agent leads him into a plot to strike at the heart of the UK…

…But who can he trust?

The Colonel – the loud and overbearing Department head?

Major Green – the dashing war hero with the dedicated team?

…or Normanby – the prim bureaucrat with dark secrets in his past?

A LITTLE BOOK OF STRANGE TALES

By

RICHARD HINCHLIFFE

Come with us on a journey that will take you from the coldest reaches of outer space to the burning pit of Hellfire in this little collection of short stories and poems…